W9-AVD-973

THE
SNOWSTORM

To Peter — J. R.
For Katie Bowgen, with much love — H. C.

This translation has been sponsored by the Danish Arts Council
Committee for Literature. The publisher wishes to thank John Mason for
his work on the translation of the story and the Danish Arts Council for
their generous support.

STATENS
KUNSTRÅD
DANISH ARTS COUNCIL

Barefoot Books
2067 Massachusetts Ave
Cambridge, MA 02140

© Gaïa Editions
Text copyright © 1980 by Jørn Riel
Illustrations copyright © 2012 by Helen Cann
The moral rights of Jørn Riel and Helen Cann have been asserted

First published in the United States of America by
Barefoot Books, Inc in 2012
All rights reserved

Translation by John Mason
Graphic design by Graham Webb, Design Principals, Warminster, UK
Color separation by B & P International, Hong Kong
Printed in China on 100% acid-free paper
This book was typeset in Avenir and Cleanhouse
The illustrations were prepared in watercolor, graphite and collage

ISBN 978-1-84686-797-2

Library of Congress Cataloging-in-Publication Data is available
under LCCN 2012009599

1 3 5 7 9 8 6 4 2

THE
SNOWSTORM

Written by Jørn Riel

Illustrated by Helen Cann

Translated by John Mason

Barefoot Books
Step inside a story

Contents

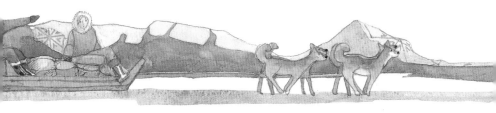

1. Springtime in Kigatak

One day, when Leiv was up on the mountain looking at his fox traps, he noticed a pair of black ravens swinging in huge circles along the rock face. Suddenly one of them tucked in its wings and plummeted down in a terrifying dive. Just before it hit the ice, it spread its wings again and climbed upward in great spiraling arcs. He knew it was the ravens' mating ritual, and it meant that spring was on its way.

These days, it seemed to Leiv as though the Iceland of his childhood was part of a story that belonged to someone else. His family was his friends, Apuluk and Narua, and their people. His home was the settlement they had built for the winter, in the north of Greenland at a place called Kigatak.

For a time it had seemed that life would never go back to normal after he and his friends were driven north by Viking raiders and separated from Thorstein and the farmstead at Stockanæs, where they had lived for the past year. The Inuit had helped them defeat the terrible raider brothers, Grimur and Rane, and had welcomed Leiv, Sølvi and Frida to their settlement, despite the differences between them.

When Leiv spoke Icelandic, his mother tongue, with Sølvi these days, he often had to search for the right words. The Inuit language came more naturally to him now. Little Frida, mute since birth, was adapting to her new life too, glad to still have Sølvi with her to protect her. Sølvi had hidden Frida from Viking raiders, who had destroyed her father's farmstead and killed her mother and everyone else who lived at Stockanæs. As for Frida's father, Thorstein, no one had heard from him since before the raid. But Frida was well cared for at the settlement. Old Shili, the shaman, had taken a shine to her and was looking after her as if she were his own child.

The group had spent the winter in peace and plenty, despite the reports of raiding pirates further off along the coast. They had food in abundance and the new homes they had built were warm and comfortable. Leiv loved the peace, but he longed to know more about the unexplored lands further north. The sight of the ravens brought thoughts of journeying to those far lands back to his mind.

He often thought about Thorstein too. Thorstein was Frida's father, and the reason Leiv had left his own father's farm. Thorstein had killed Leiv's father, but then he had looked after Leiv and his friends when they were shipwrecked and alone. Where was he? Could he have been sailing north when the raiders attacked and destroyed the farmstead?

At sunset that day, Leiv went to Shinka, Apuluk and Narua's grandfather, who knew almost everything there was to know about everything. Shinka knew the history of the Inuit, and he had told Leiv that long ago, the Inuit people had come to Greenland from the west.

Leiv sat down on the old man's sleeping bench and asked his question. "Shinka, where do people come from?"

The old man took a deep look at Leiv before speaking. "In the beginning the world was inhabited only by two men. They were both great shamans with many spirits to help them, and they had a burning desire to see more people in the world. So one of them turned himself into a woman. After that they bred many children, and that's how humans came into being."

Leiv shook his head. "That wasn't what I meant," he said. "I meant how did people come to Greenland?"

Shinka smiled. "Well now, that's quite a different question. In our stories, we often talk about how people came from the other side of the sea. That is probably where we all come from, for the land we now call Inuit Nunat, the Land of Humans, was completely uninhabited by Inuits before us. On the other side of the sea there are also Inuits, and in many ways they are like us."

"But," continued Leiv, "how far did people have to sail to get here across the sea?"

"Ah," replied Shinka, "it was not far, and so they had no need to sail at all. Way up north there is a narrow strait that is frozen most of the year. You can drive across it with a dogsled. Where my father once crossed, you could see easily from one coast to another. You could travel between the two lands in less than a day. That was what my father told me, and why would he not tell the truth?"

"Where is this narrow strait?"

"I am not entirely sure for I have never been there myself. But they say that it is so far north that it is completely dark for half the year, then light for the other half."

Leiv thanked Shinka and returned to his own sleeping bench. He pondered what Shinka had told him. He knew that, as you traveled north, the days grew longer and longer in summer, and shorter and shorter in winter. If there were six months of light and six months of dark, the strait must lie as far north as you could go. What would it be like to get so far north

11

that you could cross the strait and meet all those people who lived over there, even if some of them were enemies? Leiv had heard Apuluk's father speak of other Inuits living on the other side of the sea — hostile people he called "Erkiliks." But if they were Inuit, how could they be warlike? It made no sense to Leiv. He had to see for himself.

If only he could get Apuluk to go with him on this journey. He probably wouldn't be able to do it alone. Leiv settled down under the skins on the sleeping bench he shared with Apuluk, Narua and Sølvi, his sealskin clothes hanging from the drying rack above his head. He fell fast asleep.

The Inuits had amassed large stocks of meat, which they could draw upon during the winter months. By the time the ice had formed, most species of seal had left for the open sea, with only the small jar seals remaining in the fjords. They regularly caught such seals through their breathing holes, but it was only natural for days or even weeks to pass without any major catch, and then they had to rely on their reserves.

With the help of the children's father, Apuluk and Leiv had found a place to store meat just an hour's journey from the settlement. The day after Leiv's conversation with Shinka, the two friends harnessed the dogs and drove out to fetch meat. A pale sun was hanging low in a completely cloudless sky, and it was freezing so hard that the dogs' breath left tongues of white steam in the air.

They found the spot and, with great effort, rolled away the heavy rock that kept wild animals away from the meat. Everything inside was, of course, frozen into a solid lump, and the boys had to use small rocks to hack away the pieces of meat.

Both seals and birds were stored here, the seals piled with their blubber sides touching, which made it easier to cut them free.

When they had loaded the sled and carefully resealed the meat cache, they headed home. Leiv ran alongside the sled with one hand on the upright stanchion. "What do you think I should say to Shili?" he asked Apuluk. "He so much wants to adopt Frida, but he can't, can he? Not as long as we aren't sure whether Thorstein is alive."

"Why not?" Apuluk looked at him in surprise.

"Because, if he returns home, Thorstein will want her back, of course."

Apuluk shouted at the dogs to pull the sled further toward the coast. "As long as Thorstein is away," he said, "Shili can take his place. Among us it is not unusual for children to be adopted even though their parents are alive."

"That's not how it is for the northmen," replied Leiv. "And Frida is still a northman. If only I knew whether Thorstein was alive or not."

"You can ask Shili," was Apuluk's advice. "He is the only person who can tell you."

So Leiv did just that. Shili could both hear and see things that ordinary people could not. When they returned with the meat, Leiv went over to Shili with a tender rump of young seal and asked his question. The old shaman sighed heavily.

"I understand why you want to know whether Frida's father is dead or alive," he said. "But I cannot give you the answer."

"Can't you try?" asked Leiv.

"I am old," replied Shili, "and I have none of the power of youth. But I could, of course, try to ask the helping spirits. They might come to our aid."

2. Spirits from Another World

Everyone in the communal house watched excitedly as the preparations for the ritual were made. Old Shili had himself tied hand and foot with long cords. He was placed on his sleeping bench in a sitting position and one by one the lamps were extinguished.

The youngest children hid behind their parents, a little afraid of this dangerous summoning of spirits but too full of curiosity not to watch. And it certainly was exciting. Leiv, Apuluk, Narua and Sølvi could not see much in the darkness, but that only sharpened their hearing.

Softly Shili started to sing, and some of the elders joined in to help him. At first his voice was fragile, like that of a newborn child, but little by little it grew in strength until at last it filled the whole room with a power that had the sealskin hangings swaying.

Then suddenly they heard thundering blows begin from the great drum in the center of the floor. Of its own accord it began sending its booming rhythm into the room.

The children were trembling. They could hear Shili groaning and twisting in the ropes that bound him. Then he was crying pitifully, "I cannot do it! I cannot! I have not the strength!"

But the old men sitting around him replied, "Keep going, Shili! Keep on going!"

And they started up their singing again to help him on his perilous spiritual journey. An icy wind rushed through the house. It was a terrible wind, a wind from the unknown that made hearts shrink in terror.

"Now he is gone," whispered Narua to Sølvi. "The wind came and took him away."

The young northman girl stared in terror into the darkness. She could see some vague creatures, melting shadows that might only have been her imagination. She heard Shili's voice coming now from somewhere outside the house.

"Ah! Ah! He is alive," it said. The voice receded further and further into the distance. "Ah! He is alive. The evil must die by the knife."

"Where is he?" roared Shinka. "Where is he?"

There was a long pause before Shili answered. First they heard a fox growling down through the smoke hole above them, and they could hear that terrible wind circling over the roof, howling. Then finally Shili's voice could be heard through the noise. It was very faint, so faint they could scarcely catch it.

"To the north," it whispered. "North. Ah, the knife..."

Apuluk stirred uneasily. He felt inside his sealskin boot for the knife Thorstein had given him. Now Shili's voice disappeared entirely. Once again the floating drum was drowning out all other sound with its booming rhythm.

A fox barked again through the passage of the house, and Apuluk, feeling Sølvi pressing herself against him in her fear, reassured her.

"It's only the helping spirits," he whispered. "They won't harm us."

It took a long time for Shili's spirit to return to his body. They heard him groaning and whimpering as though he had endured the most terrible torments. Then suddenly he spoke in his normal voice, asking for the lamps to be lit and for his cords to be untied. Once he had taken a gulp of water and had rubbed his wrists and ankles to get the blood going again, he lay back exhausted.

"There was no sign of Thorstein himself," he said. "It was a journey into the unknown, but nothing was seen of Thorstein."

"But is he alive?" asked Leiv anxiously.

"He may be alive," replied Shili. "That which spoke through my mouth said he lived."

"And the knife?" Apuluk was leaning excitedly over Shili's plank bed.

Shili shook his head.

"From what my mouth has spoken we must take it that Thorstein is possessed by something evil, and that only a certain knife can kill that evil. More we do not know."

The old man now turned his back to the boys. The summoning of spirits had drained him and now he wished to rest.

Sitting on the sleeping bench that evening, the four friends could talk about nothing but Shili and the summoning of spirits.

"I wonder what he meant, about only the knife being able to kill the evil," said Apuluk.

"I think it's even more strange that he said Thorstein is up north," said Leiv. "What is he doing up there, when he sailed down to southern Greenland to take Rollo to Gardar?"

Apuluk tapped his front teeth with a fingernail. "It doesn't suit you so badly, him being up north," he laughed.

Leiv looked at him questioningly. "What do you mean?"

"Well, you're so keen to go north. Now you can look for Thorstein at the same time."

"Oh, I see." A broad smile spread across Leiv's face. "Do you want to come?"

Apuluk nodded. He closed his eyes for a moment so that he could picture the seemingly infinite expanses of land that lay to the north and west.

Narua, who was sitting on the ground alongside Sølvi, spoke next.

"If you're going on a journey, I'm coming too."

She spoke so matter-of-factly — not at all in the way that Inuit girls usually spoke. Leiv and Apuluk burst out laughing.

"Who says we want you to come with us?" Leiv teased her.

"Your sealskins say so when they need sewing, and your stomachs when you are hungry," Narua replied. She drew the silver needle that Thorstein had given her out of the hollow bone that she kept hidden in her sealskin boot and held it out in the light of the blubber lamp. Narua loved her needle. It made it so

easy for her to do all kinds of sewing, even things that had been very difficult with her old bone needles.

Sølvi was sitting on the ground with her knees drawn to her chest, softening up sealskin boots by whacking them with a kamiut stick. "You never know," she said without looking up. "You might find a use for a second girl on a journey like that."

Narua nodded enthusiastically. "But of course, you'll have to come too, Sølvi!" She looked entreatingly at her older brother.

Apuluk didn't answer. He played thoughtfully with the strap of the amulet that crossed his bare chest. Sølvi was watching him expectantly. It was Leiv who answered. "Sølvi's not used to traveling. And anyway Frida can't manage without her."

Narua slid the needle back into the hollow bone. "It'll be good for Frida to be alone with Shili. She'll learn to understand our language more quickly if she doesn't have any northmen to listen to."

"But Sølvi isn't used to traveling," Leiv repeated. "She's never been on a journey with a sled before."

"Nor had you the first time we traveled together," retorted Narua.

Apuluk got to his feet. He walked across the small room. Halfway there he turned and looked at Sølvi. "If you want to come with us, then you can ride on my sled," he said softly. His eyes rested first on Sølvi, then on Leiv.

"When do we leave?" asked Sølvi.

Leiv looked long and hard into his foster brother's eyes. Then he smiled. "As soon as we are ready," he said.

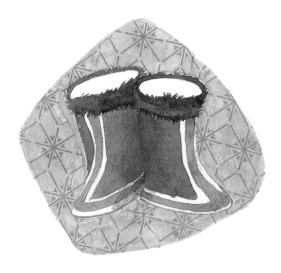

3. The Departure

Apuluk and Leiv began planning their long journey. They roped up the two sleds and gave the dogs' harness and their hunting weapons a thorough check. The girls repaired skins and sewed small sealskin shoes to put on the dogs when the ice made their paws bleed. They hammered blubber for the lamps, stacking it in blocks so it would not spill out, and packed supplies of dried meat.

By the time the new moon rose, the little expedition was ready to set off. It was a sunny morning. The cold bit viciously at their cheeks, but the snow was hard and easy to drive on. Sølvi rode on Apuluk's sled and Narua on Leiv's. They rode away from the settlement without any great fuss, as is the way with Inuits, who took off when the impulse came upon them and returned when the journey was at an end.

The snow buntings had just arrived on Greenland. Even though the birds had come very early that year, and even though there was still a hard frost, it felt as though their arrival heralded spring. Now they would be traveling with these tiny birds to the northernmost part of Greenland.

Everywhere the landscape was covered in snow. The ice lay thick and firm on the fjords, and the sleds glided quickly and easily across a snow crust beaten hard by many powerful winter storms.

For Sølvi, this sled ride into the unknown was a fairy tale. Barely sixteen, she had never in her life traveled by sled, and so there was no end to the awe she felt at the power of the dogs or at Apuluk's expertise as a driver. She leaned back against the load, far too occupied by these new and exciting experiences to feel the cold.

"You'll have to jump off the sled once in a while," Leiv shouted to her, "or else you'll start to freeze."

Sølvi nodded and called back, "I'm not a bit cold." But she jumped off the sled anyway and ran alongside Apuluk. It was wonderful running in the sealskin boots Narua had sewn for her. They had a lining of hareskin and thick soles made of oogruk, or bearded seal. Between the inner and outer sole of the boot Narua had stuffed hay, which Sølvi knew she had to dry in the evening. Otherwise the boots would become as cold as ice.

Sølvi had taught herself many things during the winter she had spent with the Inuits. And as she ran, she thought about all that had happened over the past year. First, of course, just after Thorstein had left, there had been that terrible attack on Stockanæs by those Vikings, Grimur and Rane. It had been a terrifying experience. She had seen many people killed. The only reason she and Frida were still alive was because Helga had sensed trouble and sent her out on the mountain with the child when the raiders' ship first appeared in the fjord.

She shivered as she thought of the time she had spent with Frida hiding high above Stockanæs. From the mountain, they could see the dead bodies lying between the houses. Starving and frozen, they had been in constant fear that Grimur and his brother would return. But Leiv and Apuluk had come instead, thank God.

Life with the Inuits was so completely different from the way she had lived with the northmen. At the settlement they were one large community. They had no leaders and virtually no possessions. Their catch was divided according to fixed rules, so that even those in dire straits had their share as long as the meat lasted.

To her amazement, Sølvi discovered that the Inuits did not know God.

They had other
beings, mostly spirits,
which they feared and always tried to keep
on good terms with. But at the same time, the Inuits
had a world of stories that was just as rich as that of the
northmen. Sølvi had heard many of them during the
course of the winter, when the oldest members of the
group helped pass the long, dark days and nights by
talking about the deeds of their forefathers.

Panting, she leapt back up onto the sled. Hot from the running, she pushed back the hood of her anoraq and looked across at Leiv, who was driving parallel to Apuluk.

"How strange!" she thought. "Here we are, this northman boy and I, each sitting on our sleds in this extraordinary land." She hoped they would manage to find this place that Leiv longed for.

For Sølvi, there was nothing in the least frightening about the idea of a long journey. She liked the Inuits' way of life, moving from place to place and catching every day whatever they needed. Above all, she loved her new friends. As a serf at Thorstein's farmstead, she had had no time for friends. There, life had been nothing but work and sleep. She had been treated well by Helga, but she had never been allowed to forget that she belonged to Thorstein. Even though she was now traveling with Narua, Leiv and Apuluk, she still belonged to the Stockanæs farmer. She was his possession, and he could claim her as his if ever he returned.

In the evening, the four friends pitched camp to the north of a couple of towering islands known as the Eider Islands. Apuluk told them about the large flocks of birds that gathered here in the summer. He had been here once with his parents as a little boy, but it was so long ago, he said, that Narua had been carried there in her mother's sling.

"When we pass this place on our way home," he said, "it will be full of birds."

Leiv smiled and shook his head. "Who knows?" he said. "It may be next summer before we ride past here next time. Or it may well be the depths of winter."

Narua nodded and laid a scorching hot stone in the pot. "As long as we haven't been slaughtered by the Erkiliks. If that happens, we'll never see these islands again."

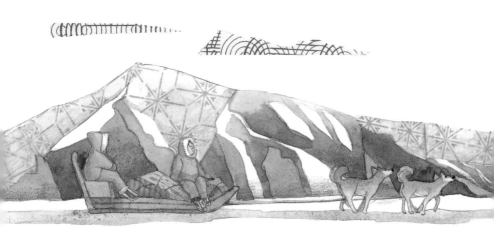

4. Following Tracks

Only a few days after their departure, Sølvi learned a lesson about how much knowledge and experience a hunter needs to move away from the security of the settlement. They were traveling across sea ice that was still solid enough to bear the sleds, though they hit drifts of heavy, soft snow from time to time. Where the snow was firm, they could move fast, but where it had been sheltered in the lee of the wind by compacted ice floes or large icebergs, they had to plow their way through. The dogs disappeared entirely under the snow, and the sleds slid slowly forward, their runners buried.

They had just driven through a large patch of soft snow one day when Apuluk signaled that they should stop. He walked a little way ahead of the sleds to make tracks for the dogs. "Bears have been here," he shouted. "Come and have a look." The other three ran over to him, and he pointed out some deep prints in the snow. "It's a mother with her cub," he explained.

Leiv studied the tracks. "Those big prints there?" he asked. "Are they the tracks of a third bear?"

Apuluk knelt down and drew a circle around a large bear-paw print. "Two adults and a cub have been here," he said. "Can you see what has happened?"

All three shook their heads, and Apuluk went on, pointing at the tracks.

"This she-bear has come out of hibernation too early. She may have been lying in a cave near one of the icebergs we just passed. Something or other has woken her up — maybe the iceberg tilted a little or

maybe it cracked. In any case, something happened
to make her venture out. She dug her way out and
must have brought her cub with her."

"Aren't the cubs bigger than that?" asked Sølvi in
surprise.

"They are about the same size as a puppy when
they are born," replied Apuluk, "and they have no fur
at all. There is nothing as defenseless as a newborn
bear cub. It is completely naked and blind and has to
be tucked under its mother straightaway so as not to
freeze to death."

"Do you think the cub died of cold when they left the den?" Sølvi was looking down at the tiny prints.

"I don't think so. Otherwise these tracks wouldn't have been here," answered Apuluk. "But a life-and-death battle has gone on here. The mother must have wandered around looking for a safe hiding place for her and her young, but then a he-bear noticed her tracks and followed her to eat the cub. He must have woken up early too. Polar bear cub is a he-bear's favorite food."

"They don't eat their own young, do they?" Sølvi shivered. "The poor mother-bear!"

Apuluk laughed. "I think you should be sorry for the he-bear instead. There's nothing as dangerous as a she-bear with young."

He pointed toward the blood-soaked tracks. "It was a terrible battle. The mother defended her young, and the he-bear was mad with hunger. But, as far as I can see, the she-bear won the day. They nearly always do."

He pointed once again to the tracks. "Yes," he said with a nod of conviction, "the he-bear was really hungry. He was thin and didn't have much strength left. Look at the tracks, the way the toes turn inward. On a fat bear they would turn out."

Apuluk followed the tracks for a few yards. "Here you can clearly see the marks of the she-bear. She has made her way out onto the drift ice, where the wolves can't get at her."

Leiv followed the he-bear's tracks in toward the land. There were red bloodstains in and beside them. "Do you think it is somewhere around here?" he asked. "How about following it, Apuluk?"

Sølvi looked at Apuluk. "Oh, yes," she said. "Let's kill it. Just think! Eating your own child!"

Apuluk fixed her with an earnest look. "A polar bear lives with the nature that it has been given," he said. "It cannot change that, any more than any of us can change the fact that we are human." He paused and then nodded his head. "But let's follow him. We can always use more fresh meat for the dogs." They returned to the sleds and fetched their weapons. Then they followed the tracks that led toward the shore and up into the foothills.

41

They caught sight of the he-bear in a hollow in the snow. When it saw the humans, it tried to get up, but no longer had the strength. It just stretched out its long neck, waving its head from side to side and roaring at them in fury. Blood was seeping slowly from its mouth, which had been ripped open right up to its left ear.

"A she-bear defending her cubs must be a terrible foe," whispered Narua.

Gripping his harpoon in both hands, Apuluk carefully approached the animal. He drove the weapon deep into its heart, and the bear fell back with a loud cry.

"If you are ever attacked by a she-bear with cubs, Leiv," he said, "you must go for the mother first. If you kill the cub before the mother, you are almost guaranteed to be killed yourself. Almost nothing can stop a she-bear defending her young."

While Apuluk and Sølvi skinned the bear and cut it up, Narua and Leiv went back for the sleds. Before long they had loaded the fresh meat on top of the rest of their equipment and were ready to continue their journey.

"There'll be a feast for the dogs this evening," said Sølvi. "And it was a good thing you killed it, Apuluk, because I think it was in terrible pain."

Apuluk nodded. He patted the new bearskin they were sitting on. "His suffering is over," he said. "Now he will help us. We can use this as an extra sleeping skin."

5. The Storm

After many days of traveling — they couldn't tell how many as none of them kept track of time — they were caught unawares by a storm. It came upon them suddenly, as spring storms do, the only warning being the few minutes in which the snow blows into low-lying drifts.

Apuluk waved to Leiv, who was driving behind him, and shouted that he should quickly unharness the dogs and look for shelter.

But Leiv couldn't hear, and before he could catch up with his friend, a powerful blast was upon them. Narua, who like her brother had understood what these heavy gusts of wind meant, immediately reined in the dogs. She leapt down and slipped the traces off the lead strap on the sled so the dogs could find cover from the drifting snow. As she stood with the bundle of traces in her hands, she was struck by a gust so strong that she was blown off her feet.

Leiv threw himself on top of her as though to press her down on the ice. "What do we do?" he yelled. He was at a total loss, casting around for Apuluk only to have his eyes blinded by snow.

"Turn away from the wind!" screamed Narua. "This is just the start. It'll get much worse." She gripped Leiv by the hand, and they both turned their backs to the storm. "We have to try to turn the sled over," she shouted in his ear, but he couldn't hear her.

"Turn the sled over! Turn! The sled! Over!" she yelled at the top of her voice, gesturing until Leiv nodded to show he had understood. He dropped to his knees, crawled over to the sled and grabbed hold of the stanchion.

Then a mighty gust of wind hit him, half lifting the sled off the ice. Straining every muscle, Leiv managed to turn it over on its side, heavy load and all. It skidded on a few yards before stopping with the stanchion buried deep in snow.

"Narua! Narua!" yelled Leiv.

"I'm here, behind you," she yelled back. "We must try to shovel snow up on the windward side."

They piled snow over the sled with their bare hands until the open triangle formed by the stanchion and the far end of the runner was completely covered. Then they crawled into the shelter created by the sled.

Narua turned to Leiv. "The dogs didn't get free of the traces. We'll have to try to release them. Otherwise they can easily be strangled."

Leiv felt for his knife and then crawled back out into the roaring storm. It flung itself upon him with all its crushing power, and he pressed himself down against the ice as hard as he could to stop himself from being lifted up and blown away. Between blasts of wind, he inched his way on his stomach toward the spot where they had left the dogs. They were still in their traces, which were tangled as they always were during a sled run.

They were lying in a tight cluster, their heads buried under their bushy tails, and they whined with joy when they smelled him close by. Leiv worked his way into the center of the pack and began undoing the traces, which were attached to the reins with bone pegs set into little rings of bone. Once he had finished, he dragged in the long ropes and bound them around his waist so they would not blow away. Then he tried to work his way back to the sled and to Narua, but everything was a white whirl of snow, and his tracks were completely covered. He had a sense of the direction he ought to

crawl in, but he had no idea whether it was right. To make sure he was not moving too far away, he would stop occasionally and try to listen. Suddenly he caught Narua's voice through the howling storm. It was not coming from ahead of him at all.

Leiv leapt up and stumbled toward the sound, but the voice was drowned again in the roar of the gale and the shriek of the snowstorm. The wind blew him off his feet and rolled him through the snow. His mouth was choked with drifted snow, and he felt as though he were slowly suffocating when he finally struck something hard. Gasping, he reached out both hands and grabbed hold of the outer edge of the sled's runner.

"Leiv! Leiv!" came Narua's voice.

"Here!" he screamed in desperation. "By the runner!"

Narua leaned out of the opening, which she had kept free of snow, and felt with her hand along the runner until she found one of Leiv's boots.

"You can let go now," she shouted. "I've got you."

Leiv let go of the runner and turned so that he could grip Narua's hand. Slowly he managed to drag himself in under the sled. There he lay for a long time gasping and struggling for breath. He was hardly aware of Narua stripping off his outer skins.

"You mustn't get wet," she said, "for we haven't got a fire to dry clothes by."

Leiv sat up as best he could under the low ceiling. He pulled off his sealskin trousers and handed them to Narua, who meticulously brushed all the snow off them. "Crawl in under the skins," she said, "or you'll get cold."

While Leiv had been fetching the traces, Narua had cut the sleeping skins free of the load and spread them out under the sled. Leiv crept in between the skins, and, once Narua had removed all the snow from both his clothes and hers, she crept in beside him.

"You ought to take your clothes off like I've done," she said, "and lay them under the sleeping skin. That'll get the damp out of them and it will stop them from getting stiff."

Leiv did as she said, and soon they were lying between the thick skins under the sled and keeping each other warm.

"I've got a strange heavy feeling in my head," he said.

Narua nodded. "That's quite common," she said. "Lots of people feel like that when there's a storm. It feels as though the hood of your anoraq were tied too tight."

Leiv thrust his knife up into the base planks of the sled. "I wonder what's happened to Apuluk and Sølvi," he asked.

Narua laughed. "They'll probably manage better than us. They've got the bags of provisions with them."

Narua was right. As soon as Apuluk had felt the first gust of wind, he had steered for the shore. He came to a halt close to a large snow drift. He let the dogs loose from their traces and shouted to Sølvi, "See if you can upend the sled so it doesn't blow away!"

Sølvi did as she was told without asking any questions. She managed to push the sled over on its side and, after many attempts and helped by the gusting winds, at last she tipped it upside down. She

lay down under it and waited for Apuluk. When the sled was covered in snow, she began to be afraid that he had been blown away. After an eternity, she heard his voice and saw a hole being kicked in the wall of snow. "See if you can squeeze through the hole," he shouted. "Take my hand and don't let go."

Sølvi got through the hole easily and was out in the open. The weather was appalling. It was one mass of whirling whiteness, a whining, roaring hell of snow that drove thousands of needles into her face. She clung to Apuluk's hand and allowed herself to be pulled across the ice. Apuluk let her go, and she scraped the snow from her eyes. She found herself in a small cave that Apuluk had dug in the snow drift. It was just high enough to allow her to sit upright, and long and wide enough for both of them to lie down outstretched. She turned happily toward Apuluk, but he had already disappeared out into the storm.

This time it was not so long before he returned. He passed the sleeping skins and sacks of provisions in to her and then came in himself. Once he had brushed all the snow off, he walled up the entrance. He left a little triangle open in one upper corner, which he called their "nose".

Sølvi spread out the skin of the freshly killed bear as an underlay, then laid the large stitched quilts of reindeer skin on top. "Where are Narua and Leiv?" she asked anxiously.

"They'll manage," he replied. "Narua knows what to do." He pushed the sack of provisions up against the wall.

"How long do you think the storm will last?" asked Sølvi.

Apuluk shook his head. "It's hard to know," he replied. "Two days, three perhaps."

"Three days?" Sølvi looked around the tiny cave. "Do we have to stay here for three days?"

Apuluk laughed. "Yes, unless you prefer to be out there. Here we are safe. We can sleep and keep warm and we even have food to eat." He rummaged around in the sack of provisions and took out his fire drill.

Sølvi watched in amazement as he spun the drill and, in no time at all, turned the glowing wood of the base into tiny blue flames in the dried moss. Soon his lamp was dancing with yellow flames that threw out both light and heat.

"Are you hungry?" asked Apuluk.

Sølvi shook her head. "Not really. It's probably best to save our supplies. But I am tired and my head feels funny."

"It's the storm," said Apuluk. "Let's go to sleep." He stripped off all his clothes and crawled in naked between the skins.

Sølvi sat for a while gazing thoughtfully into the lamp. Of course she had seen naked people before, and she had also been naked with others. In the bathhouse at Stockanæs, boys and girls had bathed together, and the Inuits had also been naked in the communal area at the winter settlement because it often got so warm indoors. By the same token, they had slept without clothes all through this journey because the skins were warmer if you lay between them naked. But then they had been together, all four of them. Now it was just Apuluk and her.

It seemed that she and Leiv lacked the easy naturalness that Narua and Apuluk had with their bodies. It was as though they were a little ashamed of being naked.

Apuluk raised his head and smiled at her. "Aren't you tired?" he asked.

Sølvi nodded. Then, suddenly resolute, she took off all her clothes and laid herself down beside Apuluk. She lay there on her back in complete silence without moving a muscle. She could feel the warmth building under the reindeer skins, trapped by the hollow hairs of the hides.

When Apuluk rose and turned out some of the wicks in the lamp to save blubber, she noticed for the first time how finely built he was. And without thinking about what she was doing, she reached out a hand and let it glide over his back.

Apuluk turned and looked at her, his eyes full of questions. Taking her hand, he lay down again under the skins and was soon asleep.

Sølvi was filled with a sense of security. No northman boy, apart from Leiv, had ever been as good to her as Apuluk was. When she was with him, everything became such a pleasure, such fun. She stretched and turned toward him. He mumbled something incomprehensible in his sleep and laid one arm heavily across her chest.

It took a long time for Sølvi to fall asleep.

All the following day they remained lying there between the skins and talking. Sølvi told Apuluk about her life. She had been born on some islands that she called the Færoes. They were quite a long way south of Iceland, which is itself to the south of Greenland. She could not remember much about these islands, for she and her mother had been carried off by English pirates when she was four. What most stuck in her mind was the pirate captain, who had been as big as a bear with a long greasy beard divided into a mass of thin braids.

She and her mother had been carried to Norway, where they were sold as serfs to a rich tradesman, who immediately sold them on to an Icelandic farmer. For seven years she had been a serf at his farm. Then her mother had died, and she was sold again to Thorstein at Stockanæs. There she became the nursemaid for Frida, who had just been born. Since she was a serf, she was forced to go with them to Greenland when Thorstein was banished for killing Leiv's father.

Apuluk listened to all this in silence, waiting to speak until she had finished. "But surely they can't sell people!" he said heatedly.

Sølvi nodded. "Yes, you can on Iceland and many other places in the world. Every year there are many people who are caught and sold as serfs."

Apuluk stared up at the snow ceiling. "Was your mother from the Færoes too?" he asked.

"No. She was born in England. My father was from the Færoes and, when he married my mother, she went there with him, far out across the sea. My father was killed when the pirates attacked his farm and captured me and my mother."

Apuluk turned and searched her face. "I don't get it," he said, "so maybe I'm a bit slow. But how can a person who is free be someone else's serf?"

"That's just how it is," replied Sølvi. "And I am still Thorstein's serf. I am his property, and he can sell me and treat me as he pleases."

Apuluk glanced up at the knife that he had buried in the snow wall. "If I kill Thorstein and steal you, then will you be my property?"

Sølvi nodded. "Yes, but Thorstein and Helga have always been good to me. It wasn't difficult being a serf at Stockanæs."

"But he owns you just as…" Apuluk pointed at the oil lamp. "Just as that belongs to me?"

"Yes, I belong to him. Only he can give me back my freedom." Sølvi gave him a sidelong look. "Would you like to own me, Apuluk?"

Apuluk thought long and deep before answering. "Not as a serf. For my people there are no serfs. We are all free and can decide for ourselves."

Sølvi found his hand under the skin. "I would like you to own me, Apuluk," she said in a soft voice, "even if I had to be your serf."

"If Thorstein dies, are you free then?" asked Apuluk.

"Then Frida will inherit me. Then I'll belong to her."

"My wish is that you should be free," said Apuluk. He gave her hand a gentle squeeze and got up to enlarge the little air hole in the wall.

The storm passed almost as quickly as it had come. After the second night of lying buried in the snow, Sølvi woke feeling that she was freezing. She turned toward Apuluk only to discover that he was no longer there. Then she saw the hole that had been dug out to the open air and the dazzling daylight that was streaming in through it. She leapt out of the skins and squeezed herself through the hole. Outside, only fifty yards from the snow drift where they had lain, Leiv, Narua and Apuluk were digging Leiv's sled out of the snow.

Sølvi ran toward them with whoops of joy. The three of them turned and stared at her in amazement. Then they all began to hoot with laughter. "Have all your clothes been blown away, Sølvi?" asked Leiv, laughing.

Sølvi stopped in her tracks and looked down at herself. She was still naked, as she had been under the skins. All aglow with the joy she felt, she had no sense of the cold at all. She began to laugh too, and to Leiv's amazement began dancing around in the hard-packed snow. Never before had Sølvi felt so happy. She felt utterly free, as though she belonged to no one, and she was filled with love for Narua and Leiv and the entire world — and especially Apuluk.

"Whatever's up with her?" mumbled Leiv, perplexed. "Has the storm sent her off her head?"

"When people feel great joy," said Narua, "we have to sing and dance. That's just how we are. Our legs cannot stay still and joy pours out of our mouths in a torrent of crazy words."

Apuluk was watching Sølvi with a broad smile. "She is Inuk like Narua and me," he said to Leiv. "You are still only a northman if you can be surprised at someone who has been granted the gift of joy."

Sølvi fell over in the snow, completely dizzy from dancing and still laughing like a madwoman. Then she leapt to her feet and rushed into the cave for her clothes. She dressed, rolled the skins together and packed the sack of provisions. When she came out again, Apuluk was harnessing his dogs. She tied the sack to the stanchion and spread the skins out over the load.

The two sleds set off. Sølvi sat staring in rapture as the light grew stronger, spreading slowly downward like a giant fan over the snow-covered mountainsides. She was sitting sideways, looking out, her face to the east. Apuluk's eyes were on the dogs as they sought out the easiest route through these compact formations of ice. Sølvi placed a hand on his back, and he turned to look back at her. Then she began to laugh all over again, and her laughter was so infectious that Apuluk could not help laughing too.

On the sled behind them, Leiv pursed his lips disapprovingly. "I think they're both off their heads, those two," he muttered.

Narua made no reply. Instead she pulled her anoraq over her head, infected by the mood of her two friends, her own laughter bubbling up inside her.

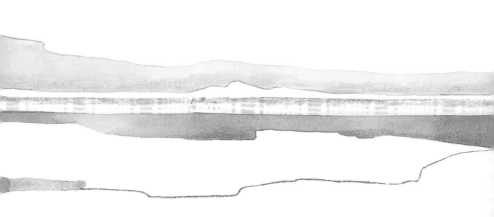

6. Contact

Nine days after the storm had abated, the little sled party reached the vast peninsula known as Nugssuaq. Here they came across a human for the first time since they had set out. They had seen a large number of Inuit tracks during their journey, but they had been old ones, and they had never followed them.

Narua was the first to notice. She shouted to Apuluk and pointed westward across the ice. Apuluk stood up on the sled and scanned the scene. Far out he could see a hunter catching seal at a breathing hole. He halted the sled and ran over to Leiv.

"Let's stay here," he said, "otherwise we'll disturb his hunting. He may have been standing there waiting for seal for hours, and, if we drive past, the seals will abandon their breathing holes."

They sat on their sleds and waited. They could see the hunter standing as if turned to stone, bent over the breathing hole with his long harpoon raised. Then all at once he struck, and a shout of joy told them that the seal had been hit. Apuluk and Leiv also gave their own cheers, and the sleds raced toward the lonely hunter.

The man belonged to a group of Inuits that neither Narua nor Apuluk had heard of. His name was Kitorak, and he had come to Greenland from the west many years before. Together with other migrants he had then traveled north, and he told them that he had spent the winter by a great sea that was frozen over for most of the year. Even though there had been many reindeer and musk oxen up there, the land had never really appealed to him. And when his tribe moved even further eastward, he had returned alone to the place where he had landed on Greenland. There he had found the group of Inuits he was now living with.

Kitorak invited them to his settlement. He told them that his group had left their winter shelters and were now traveling south, living in igloos since it was still too cold for tents. The group followed Kitorak. He had large well-fed dogs, evidence that the group had had a good winter and had not gone hungry at any point.

Once on land, they swung south and at the mouth of a narrow fjord came upon a broad thoroughfare criss-crossed with sled tracks. Now and then Kitorak would turn around, waving and shouting encouragement to them with a broad smile on a face almost blackened by the sun. Soon they came in sight of the igloos, a row of small humps that at first glance looked like random little drifts of snow. When the settlement came into sight, Kitorak let out excited shouts that brought people streaming out of the igloos, excited to see what the hunter had brought back. Their faces showed great surprise at the sight of the two foreign sleds. Their amazement was greater still when the sleds came close enough for them to see the people on them. Apuluk and Narua were familiar enough,

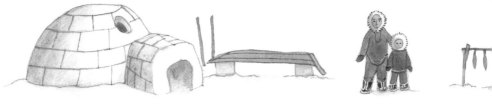

but Leiv and Sølvi attracted a great deal of attention. Many of the children ran back into their igloos and peered fearfully out from behind the skin hangings in the doorways.

They came to a stop on the shore in front of the settlement, where Kitorak told his fellow clansmen about their meeting on the ice. He pointed to Leiv and Sølvi, saying that even though they looked different, there was no reason to fear them. Leiv, he said, was almost like a proper human. He spoke their language and behaved like an Inuit. The girl with the fair hair was a bit stranger. She spoke like a child, but she was friendly and full of laughter.

The people stood for a long time observing the foreigners in silence. There was nothing suspicious about Narua and Apuluk. They looked exactly like other humans. But they were far from comfortable with Leiv. His hair made him look like a very

old man, and his eyes were the blue of freshwater ice. He was terribly tall and had a serious, almost somber look.

They were even more awestruck by Sølvi. Like Leiv, her hair was fair. But it shone like the rays of the sun. Her eyes were paler than the man's, the blue of the sky when a warm spring day stretches over the frozen ice. Her face was round and soft, and when she smiled they could see that she had beautiful white teeth and a little dimple in each cheek.

Kitorak invited the foreigners into his igloo. He told them that a guest igloo was to be built for them, but until it was finished they could stay with him. The Inuits helped to empty the sleds. Kitorak and some of the other men cut up meat for the dogs and gave them a good dinner.

Apuluk led the two dog teams down to the seashore. There he used his knife to cut a hole in a large piece of ice, through which he dragged the reins and looped them into a knot. Once the dogs were safely tethered there, he went back to Kitorak's igloo.

The igloo was full of people.

Everyone wanted to see the visitors Kitorak had found on the ice. Kitorak's wife served up boiled meat for them, keeping their mouths constantly full, which made it hard to answer the Inuits' many questions.

Before they had finished their meal, a happy commotion outside signaled that their igloo was ready. They crawled quickly out through the entrance passage, eager to see how it was possible to build a house in such a short time.

It was a cozy little igloo. Sølvi, who had never stayed in an igloo before, looked around in delight. There was a broad sleeping platform made of snow, where all four of them could sleep. The Inuits had spread out their skins, and Apuluk's traveling lamp burned in a little niche in the wall. Next to the entrance they had set in a large piece of freshwater ice that allowed the light to pour in from outside.

Kitorak, conscious that the travelers were tired after driving all night, suggested that they get a little sleep so that they could be well rested before the party that would be held that evening in their honor. He left the guest house, pushing a block of snow in front of the entrance so they could sleep in peace.

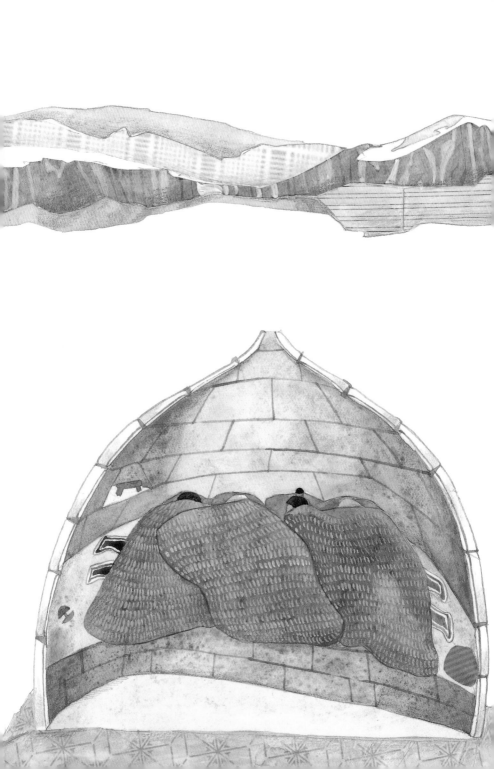

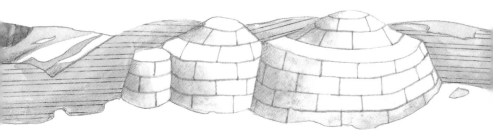

7. The Party

Sølvi awoke to the sound of many voices shouting and laughing. She got up in a daze and looked about her. Then she remembered where she was and, turning toward Apuluk, she realized that he was awake too.

"The party has started!" he said.

"Why didn't you wake us up?" asked Sølvi.

"It is our way never to wake a person who is sleeping," he replied.

"Why not?"

Apuluk rose and reached up to take his bird-skin parka, which was hanging on the drying rack under the ceiling. "Because," he said as he pulled the parka over his head, "when we sleep, we die a little. When you sleep, your soul goes on a journey, and, if you wake your body at the wrong moment, it's not certain that your soul will find its way back to it."

Sølvi nodded. It made sense, she thought.

"I also think we die a little when we sleep," she said. She pointed toward Leiv and Narua and smiled. "But now I think their souls are coming home."

Leiv stretched and uttered some strange sounds. Then he propped himself on one elbow and rubbed his eyes. "Oh, it was good to sleep a bit," he murmured.

The top of Narua's disheveled head appeared. She was lying between Sølvi and Leiv. "Do I hear drums?" she asked.

"The party started ages ago," replied Apuluk, "so we'd better be getting up."

One of Kitorak's daughters was standing outside the guest igloo waiting for them. She led them across to the party, which was taking place in a very large igloo built for the occasion. Inside they were greeted by a torrent of hospitality. They were made to sit on particularly valuable skins that had been spread on the floor, and they were expected to eat as many delicious dishes as they could manage. And there were certainly plenty to choose from. There was dried reindeer meat, seal meat in many forms — fresh, rotted, boiled and dried. There were small fish known as capelins, boiled great auk, salmon, pickled little auks, crowberries in whale oil and the contents of a reindeer stomach. There was mattaaq, or blubber, both from narwhal and from beluga, delicious boiled ribs of musk ox and frozen bear meat.

It was a magnificent feast. The clan clearly loved a good party, and, being Inuit, they seized on the slightest occasion as an excuse for major festivities — it might be the first time a child had its hair combed or took its first step, when a boy caught his first seal or, as now, when there were guests.

Apuluk and Narua and Leiv ate for all they were worth. Sølvi, for whom many of the dishes were strange, proceeded a little more carefully. Their hosts constantly urged them to eat more, and it wasn't long before Sølvi felt that she was ready to explode.

During the meal they told each other of their experiences. They talked about the weather, about the animals they had hunted and about their wanderings. When Leiv mentioned the northmen's ship, Kitorak said that they had also seen such a ship. It had been an unfamiliar and unfriendly ship with a hostile crew that had killed two of the group's best hunters. It was, he said, a large ship, and it had laid anchor for a time to the south of the settlement before setting sail again northward before the ice thickened.

"Are you sure they sailed north?" asked Leiv, full of curiosity.

"Quite sure," answered Kitorak, "for several hunters followed them at a distance in their kayaks to make sure they left the area."

"Were there people like Sølvi and me on board?" Leiv wanted to know.

Kitorak consulted some of the other hunters before replying. "Those who got close to them say that their skin was darker than yours, and that their hair was almost like the Inuits. They had a lot of hair growing on their chins, but it was either completely black or dark brown."

After several hours, the meal finally ended and the entertainment began. The men played games of strength or skill — pulling knuckles or catching hollowed rings on a sharpened bone.

Presently one of the old men took out his drum. It was a little drum compared to those used in Shili's group, and it did not have the same booming sound as Shili's, but the songs that accompanied the drumming were almost identical to those they sang at Narua and Apuluk's settlement. And, when everyone else at the party began to sing along, the two young Inuits joined in.

During the song a young hunter sprang to his feet and took up position in front of Sølvi. He danced before her, singing a witty ballad that had them all laughing out loud. Sølvi jumped up then, and she began to dance like the young hunter. She aped his movements so precisely that the laughter echoed around the room.

"She dances like one of us!" screamed the old women.

"Oh, look!" they shouted. "It's not just her legs dancing, it's her whole body! It's her arms, her throat, her eyes, her hair. She is a grand dancer."

Apuluk's eyes were fixed proudly on Sølvi, and Leiv, noticing his look, whispered to Narua. "You'd think Sølvi was Apuluk's own discovery."

Narua smiled and clapped her hands in time to the song. Before Leiv could say another word, she too had leapt up and thrown herself into the dance. All night and most of the following day they partied. When they felt tired, they lay down and slept for a few hours, and then woke again and rejoined the festivities. It was only when there was nothing at all left to eat that the party slowly ebbed. Some of the clan went to their igloos to rest, but most of the hunters harnessed their dogs to their sleds and drove directly from the party out to their hunting grounds to fill up the empty storehouse again.

8. Northward Ho!

To the dismay of the hospitable people at Kitorak's settlement, Apuluk and Leiv wanted to leave the very day after the party.

The sun was riding high in the sky, and it was now so hot during the day that small lakes of meltwater were forming on the ice they had to drive across. That meant that they didn't have much time to waste if they were to reach the strait that Shinka had described that summer. They had been given a detailed description of the route by Kitorak, who had driven it himself, and he had alerted them to dangerous places along the route where the tide had worn the banks away, and to caves in the mountain where they could spend the night.

Early in the morning, they drove out onto the sea ice to continue their interrupted journey. To the north of the Nugssuaq peninsula, they found themselves in deep snow once again. It was hard to force their way through since the dogs sometimes disappeared completely, and the sleds were constantly getting stuck. In the beginning, they took turns leading the way and making tracks. The dogs tired quickly and every day the distances they covered grew smaller.

Apuluk was aware that it was dangerous to drive their sleds in places where the snow was very deep. He knew that it prevented the ice from being in contact with the cold night air, and that this meant that the ice could be eroded from below by the tides. It grew thin and could easily crack under their weight. That was why he insisted on going on ahead and probing the ice with his long ice pick. But the others would not have it. The hard work had to be shared equally between them, they said. It was only when Sølvi fell through the ice that he got his way. He was the one with the greatest experience, and the others had to bow to that.

They had enough on their hands keeping the dogs moving all the time anyway, partly to avoid the sled getting stuck, but also to prevent damage to the dogs' paws. As soon as the sled came to a halt, the dogs would begin to lick the snow from between their pads. As they did, they would tear away the delicate hairs on their paws without realizing it, and their paws would start to bleed and become very sore.

Before they left, the girls had sewn small sealskin boots for injured dogs to wear. But even these

presented problems. They had to be inspected at every stop, for if they were tied too tightly, the paws could easily develop gangrene. After a week of struggling through the heavy drifts, they reached an area that was almost completely bare of snow. Here the ice lay smooth and shiny as far as the eye could see.

They drove on and searched for a cave that Kitorak had suggested as a place to spend the night. The cave

was low down on the edge of the ice, a hard place to find for anyone who had not heard about it, lying protected by a rocky outcrop to the north and a long dog-toothed ridge that swung around the mouth of the cave like a bent "arm," They put the dogs inside the "arm," and, once they had unloaded the sleds, Apuluk and Leiv went off to hunt for dog meat while the girls made the cave habitable for their return.

9. Taken by Surprise

After they had spent some time looking for tracks, Apuluk found fresh reindeer droppings in the wide valley that led from the fjord up to a low-lying mountain to the east. The reindeer were clearly hungry. In several places, they had dug through two feet of snow to get down to the moss and lichen they liked to eat.

The boys followed the tracks of the herd along the valley and up to the top of the mountain, where the wind had blown the ground completely bare of snow. Here the ground was visible and everything edible had been nibbled away.

Apuluk screwed up his eyes and scanned the mountainsides below them. Suddenly he stiffened.

"Umiarssuak," he swore in amazement. "Look, Leiv! A big ship."At a bend of a creek they could see the silhouette of a ship frozen fast in the ice.

Leiv shaded his eyes from the sun. "It must have been there all winter," he said. "They were caught by the ice late in the autumn."

"Is it Thorstein's?" asked Apuluk.

"No, it's much bigger than any of his skiffs. The mast is much taller too. I have never seen that kind of ship before," replied Leiv.

"There may be people living on board," said Apuluk, looking at the ship thoughtfully.

"If there are, they must have had a dreadful winter," said Leiv. "Come on, let's go down and take a look. Maybe we can help them."

They came down the mountain and crossed the ice toward the big ship.

There seemed not to be anyone alive on board, for there was no sign of life as the boys approached. Hesitantly, they walked up close and around the bows. People had been there, that much they could see, for on the starboard side lay a load of rubbish that had been thrown overboard.

"Look!" Apuluk bent down and picked up some well-gnawed reindeer ribs. "These haven't been here many days. The marrow is still fresh and…"

That was as far as he got. At that moment the air was split open by wild shouts, and a swarm of heavily armed men leapt over the gunwales and down onto the two boys.

The fight was over quickly. Leiv did not even manage to draw his knife, and Apuluk's bow was wrenched out of his hands before he could put an arrow to the string. The boys were tied up in a brutal fashion and flung aboard the ship. Once on the deck, they were grasped by a tall, gaunt man, who threw them to the ground and clapped a pair of iron rings on their ankles.

Once they had been put in irons, they were kicked down into the hold and chained together with three other prisoners. Leiv looked up, and then gasped in astonishment. He found himself staring straight into the face of Thorstein.

"Welcome, Leiv Steinursson," Thorstein said with a crooked little smile. "I wish I was able to bid you welcome to some other place."

"Thorstein? What are you doing here? Are you a prisoner too?"

Thorstein showed him his chained feet. "I have been their prisoner since August," he said.

"Who are the other two?" Leiv craned his neck to see around Thorstein. "Is Rollo here too?"

"These are Sigurd and Helge, whom you know from Stockanæs. No, Rollo is dead. These demons killed him straight away, for they do not appear to be keen on Christians. Rollo was killed, and with him most of the men I had with me. There are only us three left."

"But how did this happen?"

Thorstein leant back against one of the ship's massive timbers. "We were at anchor in a small bay in southern Greenland and were getting fresh drinking water. It was quite a long way to the stream, and I had taken as many men as possible with me, so that we wouldn't have to go more than once. When we returned, the pirates had already captured my ship. They had killed the guards and had their own ship hidden behind a large iceberg. We suspected nothing and walked straight into the trap. They overpowered us almost without a fight."

"Why have they sailed up here?" asked Leiv.

"Because the captain is greedy. He heard that the Inuits up in the north had large quantities of skins, and he wanted to lay his hands on them. We sailed north all through the autumn, and wherever we came across Inuits, he would slaughter them and steal their skins. My men and I were forced to go with them."

"Why weren't you killed?"

"Because Sigurd and Helge are young and strong and will fetch a lot of money when they are sold as slaves in the south. As for me, they are waiting for my relatives on Iceland to pay a large ransom to set me free."

"What do you think they'll do with Apuluk and me?"

"You'll probably be spared," said Thorstein, "for you have relatives on Iceland who can pay for your release. But they'll kill Apuluk. They can't sell him."

Leiv nodded. He understood. He looked at his foster brother with a heavy heart, as he lay there trying to slip out of his shackles. Then he heard a harsh voice from up on deck bawling something in a language he did not understand.

"Who is it?" he whispered to Thorstein.

Thorstein raised his head and answered the man, who laughed, clearly pleased with the reply. Leiv looked up and caught sight of a giant with jet-black hair and a long, greasy beard twisted into a mass of long braids. The sight made him shiver, for never had he seen anything as foul and evil as this person.

"This is the captain," said Thorstein. "I told him that you were from a good family on Iceland, and that Apuluk would be worth many skins to the tribe he belongs to."

"What did he reply?"

"That you would be his serf until the ransom was paid." said Thorstein.

"And Apuluk?"

Thorstein shook his head sadly. "He said that the

Skrælling would be thrown overboard the moment he had helped free the ship from the ice."

Leiv wrapped his arms around his knees, suddenly chilled. Then he spoke in a soft whisper to Thorstein. "Narua and Sølvi are with us. We left them in a cave just a few hours from here."

"Sølvi?" asked Thorstein in amazement. "What is Sølvi doing with you? Why isn't she at Stockanæs with Helga and Frida?"

Leiv stared miserably down at his shackles. "Because Stockanæs has been burnt to the ground," he replied softly. "Helga and everyone else on the farm were killed. Only Frida and Sølvi survived." Then Leiv recounted all that had happened after Thorstein had set off southward for Gardar.

Thorstein heard his story to the end without a single interruption. He sat with his lips pressed tightly together, his head leaning back against the ship's rough timbers. When Leiv had finished his story, he looked up at Thorstein to see tears flowing down over his gaunt, bearded cheeks. Thorstein's voice was no more than a whisper. "Much sorrow you have brought me with your story, Leiv. It grieves me to hear that Helga is dead."

"But Frida is alive," said Leiv.

"Yes, she is alive." Thorstein grasped his shackles and shook them. "But I doubt whether I will ever be free of these."

"Narua and Sølvi will help us," answered Leiv. "They are not so stupid as to let themselves be taken by surprise as we were."

Thorstein laughed despite himself and placed an arm around Leiv's shoulder.

"We must place our trust in God," he said, "and ask Him to lead us out of this misery."

Leiv did not reply, thinking that it would be wise in this instance to place their trust in the two girls they had left behind in the cave.

10. Narua Takes Charge

Two days passed and the boys did not come back to the cave. Narua and Sølvi assumed that they were on the track of big game and had become so engrossed in the hunt that they had forgotten all about time. To reassure her, Narua told Sølvi the story of her grandfather, who had once pursued a bear for several weeks only to be forced to give up the chase in the end when it escaped out to sea and swam away in the drift ice.

On the third day, Sølvi sensed something was wrong. She could not believe that Apuluk would become so obsessed by the hunt that he would forget about everything else. He would know that the dogs had not been fed for many days and that there was little time to spare if they were to reach the strait. Perhaps they had had an accident. She suggested to Narua that they follow the boys' tracks to see which way they had gone. Narua agreed and they left at once.

It was fairly easy for them to follow the tracks in the snow. They led across the bay at an angle and up through a valley that ended in a windswept hill. Narua quickly found the reindeer tracks the boys had been following, and she could also see that the vegetation on the top of the low mountain had been completely nibbled away.

The girls now experienced the same shock as the boys had. Sølvi grabbed Narua's arm and pointed

westward. "Look over there!" she whispered excitedly. Narua looked and saw the big ship, whose mast pointed at the sky like a warning finger. She felt at once that this ship was evil, just as Grimur and Rane's ship had been.

"Someone is coming," hissed Sølvi. The girls dropped to the ground and made themselves as invisible as possible. They saw a group of men clamber down from the ship and onto the ice. Five of them were carrying a heavy chain between them.

"It's a slave ship," exclaimed Sølvi in horror. "My mother was chained just like that with a ring around her leg."

The line of men tramped down to the nearby ice floe and began to chop out blocks of ice. To their horror, the girls recognized Leiv and Apuluk's bearskin trousers.

"They have been captured," wailed Sølvi, "and now they'll be carried off to England and sold as slaves."

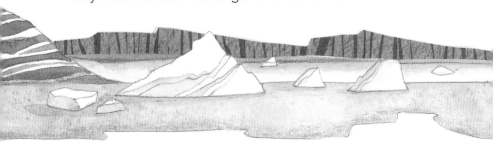

Narua lay still as stone observing the icebound ship. "We will free them," she murmured between her teeth. "Come on, Sølvi. Now we know where they are, and we know that they won't be carried off anywhere as long as the ship is trapped in the ice. We'll go back to the cave and make a plan."

"I only hope they don't find the cave," said Sølvi, as they walked through the wide valley.

"They won't. They won't be able to see either the cave or the dogs. We'll have to tie something around the dogs' mouths so they don't start howling," said Narua. She looked furiously behind her. "They are evil, those people who have captured them. The most difficult thing will be to get those irons off the boys, for they say iron is terribly strong."

"I think I can remember how the chain is attached," said Sølvi. "It goes through all the prisoners' shackles and is then fastened to a big bolt in the mast."

The girls set off at a fast pace, thinking of Leiv and Apuluk, imprisoned now as pirates' serfs. And fury welled up inside Sølvi.

"They should be killed, the whole lot of them," she burst out angrily.

Narua nodded. She was striding so fast that Sølvi had difficulty keeping up.

"They will be killed," she replied, her voice almost unrecognizable.

Sølvi looked at her and realized that Narua's fury was just as great as her own.

"But how are we going to do it?"

Narua came to an abrupt halt. Her eyes were dark with anger as she spoke. "I know what we have to do," she answered.

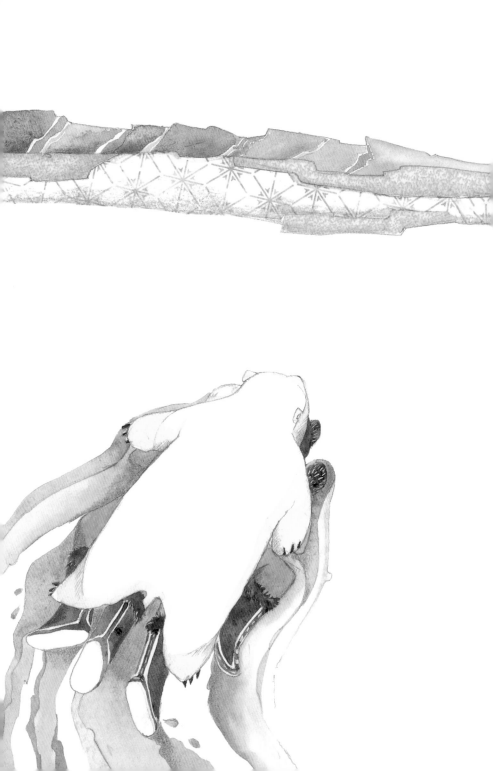

11. Free at Last

Inch by inch, Narua and Sølvi crept toward the pirate ship. They were flat on their stomachs under a bearskin, and they pulled themselves forward using knees and elbows so as to be as invisible as possible. Narua never stopped murmuring strings of incomprehensible words, which, she had explained to Sølvi, were incantations that would bring magical forces to their aid.

Even though it was nighttime, it was completely light. It was a flat light, almost lifeless, without shadows, and it made everything on the ice merge together.

It took them several hours to crawl across the bay and into the creek where the ship was lying. Once in a while they halted and lay still, waiting and listening.

If they could not hear any suspicious noises, they continued, but if they heard the slightest creaking of the ship's timbers or any sighing of the ice, they stopped dead in their tracks until everything went quiet again. Sølvi was pushing a small bowl of burning oil before her, and Narua was dragging a large sack with oil and blubber and the heavy soapstone lamp.

They stopped just a few yards away from the side of the ship and lay completely still. Sølvi explained to Narua in a whisper where the various sections of the ships were. "Over there under the little raised section the crew and the captain sleep," she whispered. She pointed from under the skin. "In the center of the ship there's a kind of well. That's the hold, and that's where the slaves are. They are chained, but I'll deal with the chain."

She fell silent and pointed up at the gunwale. Narua looked up and caught sight of a man who had risen to his feet on the deck and was now yawning and stretching. He walked across to the hold and looked down. Then he gave another long, deep yawn and settled himself on the gunwale with his back against the rigging that held up the mast.

"How do we deal with him?" whispered Sølvi.

Narua smiled and drew out the soapstone lamp. "When I was small, I was always better at throwing than Apuluk and the other boys."

It soon looked as though the guard had fallen asleep. He sat there, hunched up, supported by the rigging. A large axe lay in his lap between his loose fingers.

"Stay here!" whispered Narua. They were so close to the ship that they could clearly see the man's profile. Without a sound Narua slid out from under the skin and across the ice. In her sealskin clothes she looked exactly like a young ringed seal dragging itself across to its breathing hole.

When she was about a yard from the railing, she rose to her feet without a sound and swung the heavy lamp upward with all her strength. The lamp sailed through the air and hit the guard on the side of the head with a dull thud. He collapsed with a sigh and, fortunately, remained hanging there in the taut sails. The lamp fell back down onto the ice with a loud crack.

Narua leapt under the gunwale and stood there stock-still. But no one on board reacted to the noise made by the lamp. When she was certain that everyone was asleep, she picked up her lamp and signaled to Sølvi that she should come quickly to the side of the ship. Without a word, the two girls helped each other to clamber on board.

It was exactly as Sølvi had said. Down in the open hold, the prisoners lay sleeping. They were covered by some old skins, and the girls could hear the chains rattle every time one of them moved.

Narua crept forward with Sølvi's bowl of burning oil. The crew were sleeping under an overhanging roof, and she quietly gathered anything she

could see that would
burn — a large,
rough-spun
piece of cloth,
some rope, a
bit of canvas and a
barrel with thick black
liquid, which she tipped
over the deck. She worked almost soundlessly, only
pausing when one of the pirates stirred in his sleep.

Once she had placed everything in front of their
sleeping quarters, she poured whale oil and the
pounded blubber over it and set fire to the pile in
several places. Slowly the fire spread. It caught on the
whale oil in small leaping bursts, and Narua stood and
watched, her heart beating as the yellow flames grew
taller and taller.

Sølvi was busy too. First, she grabbed the axe
that lay between the guard's hands. He murmured
something incomprehensible when she forced his
fingers open, and for a moment he opened his eyes

and stared at her without focusing. For safety's sake, she smacked the side of his head with the flat of the axe, whereupon he slumped again. Then she jumped down into the hold. Apuluk woke on hearing the soft bump and immediately understood the situation. He sat up and pointed backward. Sølvi smiled at him and nodded. She followed the long chain until she came to the bolt that attached it to the mast. Taking careful aim, she knocked out the iron pin and released the chain.

In the meantime, Apuluk had woken the other prisoners, and they began gently pulling in the chain and drawing it out through the rings of their shackles. As soon as Leiv, Apuluk and Thorstein were free, they leapt to the stern, where they knew their weapons were kept. They had only just picked up their bows and knives when all hell broke loose on the forecastle.

The fire suddenly took hold. It was due not so much to the blubber as to the half-barrel of pitch that Narua had poured out on the deck, unaware of just how flammable the black substance was. The tar warmed up and burst into flame, sending long red tongues licking toward the sky. The ship's dry timbers soon caught fire, and before long there was a wall of flame between the forecastle and the hold.

Terrified roars were coming from the crew's sleeping quarters. "They are from England," said Sølvi to Apuluk as they stood together in the stern next to the great steering oar. "They speak my mother's tongue."

Apuluk nodded. He had his bow drawn, an arrow pointing at the fire. "They are evil," he said, "and they must die."

The uproar behind the fire was terrible to hear. With piercing screams two pirates burst through the flames and onto the deck. One was immediately stopped in his tracks by an arrow that buried itself deep in his chest, but the other made it through the flames. Howling, sword in hand, he leapt at Narua where she stood at the front edge of the hold. Leiv let loose his arrow and struck the man in the shoulder, but that did not stop him. With a maddened roar, he lifted his sword and was about to cut Narua down when once again her heavy lamp flew through the air. It struck him

with crushing force in the center of his forehead, and the roar faded into an ugly grunt. The man sank to his knees, toppled forward and fell headfirst into the hold.

Another pirate leapt through the flames, but he missed his footing and tumbled head over heels. Thorstein grabbed the man's arm, but the pirate struck back at him and they wrestled together until Thorstein was able to wrench the sword out of his opponent's hands. Then Thorstein lifted the heavy chain in his hands and brought it down on the pirate with a terrible crash.

They could hear the men on the other side of the fire coughing and screaming, suffocated by the poisonous black smoke billowing up from under the deck, when suddenly they all poured out through the smoke at once. They were a terrible sight, their faces completely blackened by soot and smoke, their eyes wild and bloodshot. But their desperation made them dangerous. Sølvi was petrified when she saw them. She let out a shriek and clutched Apuluk's arm. "That man! The big one with the beard! That's the man who kidnapped us!"

Apuluk looked at the gigantic captain, saw the smoke-blackened face with its evil red eyes, the powerful body, the thick bare arms and the huge chest. He saw how all the greasy braids of his beard danced against his chest as the giant leapt through the fire, sending sparks flying on all sides.

The captain cast around for a moment. Then with long, catlike movements he leapt toward the ship's stern, his sword whirling above his head as he roared a constant stream of oaths and curses at his attackers. Apuluk drew back his bow to snapping point and sent an arrow straight through the man's wrist as he rushed forward, making his sword fall to the deck with a clatter. But the giant plowed on with the arrow through his wrist toward the steering oar and Apuluk.

Apuluk stood his ground. He had drawn Thorstein's knife, and, as the pirate leapt at him, made no attempt to move out of his way. In fact, it looked to Sølvi as if Apuluk was stepping right into the arms of the pirate. The hand with the knife slipped under the pirate's arm, and, as the huge man tried to crush every bone in Apuluk's body, the boy drove the knife deep into his side and struck him in the heart.

For a moment the giant stood gaping in astonishment. Then the frenzy drained from his eyes. He attempted to speak, but all that came out were gargling sounds deep in his throat. His hands slowly released Apuluk and he took a couple of stumbling paces backward, staring all the while in disbelief at the boy. Then he fell on his hands and knees, coughed weakly and then collapsed onto his side, dead.

Apuluk looked down at the knife in his hands, and he thought back to what old Shili had said during the summoning of spirits.

More pirates had been trying to force their way onto the quarterdeck, but Leiv stood there with the sword that Thorstein had thrown up to him and held them at bay. Three pirates had made it onto the deck and were closing in on Leiv. One of them tried to sneak behind him, but before he could get behind the mast, he sank to his knees with a cry of astonishment, struck by Narua's lamp.

The other two pirates whirled around, and one of them lashed out at Narua. She sprang backward behind the mast, grabbing an ice pick as she did so. Before the pirate could raise his sword, she had cast the pick like an Inuit casts a harpoon, and the heavy iron shaft buried itself in the man's chest. With a roar of horror the last of the pirates sprang overboard. He fell over on the ice but quickly got to his feet again and began to run away from the ship.

Apuluk slid his knife into his sealskin boot and grasped his bow. He placed an arrow on the string and was just about to send it flying when he felt a hand on his shoulder. "Let him run, Apuluk." It was Thorstein, who had climbed up from the hold. He was bleeding a little from the blow to his chest. "Out there he may find a worse punishment than if we kill him here," he said.

Apuluk lowered the bow and looked thoughtfully at the farmer. He understood what Thorstein was asking — that he should spare this man's life. He turned to Sølvi. "Tell Thorstein that if he wants to spare the life of this evil man, I want a life in return." Sølvi translated, and once Apuluk had seen Thorstein nod, he continued. "I ask you for Sølvi. She is your serf."

Sølvi translated and Thorstein replied, "Sølvi is yours if you wish to have her."

"I do not wish to own her. But I want you to give her her freedom."

Thorstein looked at Sølvi, who had translated Apuluk's words. He placed one of his bloodied hands on her shoulder. "You are free, Sølvi, and you have your own life from now on. If I could give you something better than freedom, I would gladly do so."

Sølvi was radiant with joy. "There is nothing better," she replied, and she grasped Apuluk's hand in gratitude.

The entire bow of the ship was now one great sea of flame. The fire was spreading toward the hold and long flames were licking across the afterdeck. "Where are Sigurd and Helge?" asked Leiv. In the heat of the battle they had forgotten the two men.

Thorstein looked down into the hold. There lay the two men still trying to struggle free of their chains as the fire closed in on them. When Leiv and Apuluk had

unhooked their own chains, they had clambered up onto the deck as fast as they could to help the girls without thinking of the other prisoners. Neither of the men, so weakened from their captivity that they couldn't escape on their own, had wanted to shout for help while the fight was going on above them, but now they were in danger of being burnt alive.

Leiv jumped down and released the chain, and soon the two men were standing on deck with the others. Only two of the pirates were still alive: the guard and the other man Narua had hit with her lamp. They were

brought back to life with a couple of fistfuls of ice-cold snow and were allowed to run after their mate, who had already escaped across the ice.

They all left the burning ship and walked slowly across the creek toward the low, wind-blown mountain. Before climbing up the mountain, they turned and looked back at the burning pirate ship.

"Never again will it carry slaves," said Sølvi.

Thorstein shook his head. "I know now how it is to be a slave," he said. "At the new Stockanæs I am going to build, there will be no slaves."

12. New Beginnings

The return journey to Shili's group was made across sea ice, a little way off shore. The ice along the coast was melting, and the places where the tide had eroded had now become large gaps of open water where seabirds were settled. Leiv hadn't yet given up on the idea of exploring the foreign lands in the west, but had decided he'd had enough adventure for one summer. Thorstein's wound healed quickly, and soon he was able to run behind the sleds as the others did when the going became heavy.

The weather had turned really warm, and they slept under the open skies, with only a layer of sled skins under them. Thorstein and his men grew enthusiastic about this form of travel, something they had never tried before. There was no end to their admiration for Leiv and Apuluk's skills, both in driving the sleds and in hunting seals on the ice.

Just before the fjord ice broke up, they arrived back at the settlement. Their reunion brought with it tremendous joy, especially for Frida and her father. Thorstein saw her come running out across the ice with the Inuit children to welcome the sleds. When Frida came close enough to see who the travelers were, she started shouting, "Atata! Atata!"

Thorstein rushed to her, picking her up and lifting her high above his head. As he clasped her to him, she laid her warm cheek against his beard. "She can talk!" he shouted to Leiv and Sølvi. "Did you hear her talk?"

"She is saying, 'Father! Father!'" Sølvi shouted back as she ran to Thorstein's side.

"Can you really talk now, Frida?" she asked in the Inuit tongue.

Frida nodded. "Shili taught me. He flew up to the man in the moon and fetched my voice. He says so himself."

"What's she saying?" asked Thorstein.

"She says that the shaman of the settlement has fetched her voice from the man in the moon," Sølvi translated, and then added on her own account, "and that you will have to teach her the northman language now."

As was the Inuit custom, that night a great party was held at the settlement. Everyone was invited to Shili's tent, for the shaman wished to be host for the evening. Since people knew that the old man had little luck with his hunting, they brought him small presents in the form of dried meat. They ate and ate, and then they danced, laughed and talked, and then they ate again.

In the midst of the party, Apuluk leapt to his feet.

He grasped his drum and started to sing:

Have you ever wanted to raise your voice
above the laughter and noise of the party?
Have you ever reached the night
when you feel a change take place inside?
Have you ever felt that all your dreams and desires
are too great to live inside you alone?
I never knew that I could feel this way.
I never knew I'd have these impossible thoughts.

He took up position right in front of Sølvi and stood there for a long time swaying back and forth to the beat of the drum. Then he continued his singing:

Have you ever wanted to set off
and travel for a time, for a time?
Maybe far away all by yourself,
where you'll never see another man.
Or maybe with the ones you love,
the people who are like blood in your veins.

Tonight, I want to start my life with you.

Suddenly he threw down the drum, lifted Sølvi up and carried her out of the tent. A roar of mock protest rose up among the revellers, but everyone was smiling and laughing. A rowdy crowd followed the pair out into the night. Once outside, he threw Sølvi down on his sled, which was standing there packed and harnessed, called his dogs to their places and sped away across the brittle ice.

Thorstein watched the elopement in astonishment. He did not really know if he should step in and help Sølvi, but he refrained for he had seen the smile turning the corners of her mouth up.

"Whatever's got into him?" he asked when Leiv came back inside with blood dripping from his nose from the struggle.

Leiv laughed. "He seems to have grabbed himself a wife. This is how they get married here, Thorstein."

Narua sat between Shili and her father. She looked at Leiv. "I don't suppose my brother will ever come

back," she said. "Maybe they'll come on a visit in a few years, but never to live here again."

"What?" Leiv removed the tuft of hare's skin he had stuffed up his nose to stop the bleeding.

Narua looked down at the large, flat stones of the floor and repeated Apuluk's words: "Have you ever wanted to set off and travel… Maybe with the ones you love, the people who are like blood in your veins…"

Leiv stared at her in amazement. "You mean…?"

Narua nodded, then looked in embarrassment across at the door of the tent.

With a roar Leiv leapt forward. He grasped Narua's topknot and dragged her, for all her protests and feigned howls, through the tent. Some of the young ones tried to block his way, laughing, but they were swept aside. Old Shili was chortling with joy. He slapped his thighs, nodding and beaming at Thorstein. "Eh, what joy!" he said. "What tremendous joy! Two elopements during my party!"

Outside the tent Leiv came to a halt, unsure what to do next. "Your sled is standing behind my father's tent," whispered Narua. "I have harnessed the dogs and loaded everything we need."

Breathing a sigh of relief, Leiv grabbed her hair again. "Am I doing it right?" he whispered back.

"You probably ought to look a bit more dangerous, but otherwise you're doing fine," answered Narua between her complaints and howls. With long, firm strides, Leiv dragged his happy victim across to the sled. There he flung her on top of the load and whipped up the dogs. At breakneck speed, the sled sped over the ice and out onto the fjord.

Leiv drove north. He could see a black dot far out on the ice and he knew it was Apuluk and Sølvi, who were waiting for him and Narua to catch them up.